The Brave Lion

by Diane Jackman

Illustrated by Tina Hancocks

GONDOLA

In Mrs Harper's toyshop
in the corner of the square,
the toys sat and dreamed.
Tom the soldier boy dreamed
about playing with the real
town band.

Edward the Teddy bear was thinking
about his good ideas.
Rory the lion was asleep.
Rory was always asleep.
He sometimes dreamt about
being a hero, but it was always
so tiring, he would have to
rest afterwards.

That evening, after Mrs Harper
had closed the shop,
the toys sat and waited.
The cuckoo clock on the shelf
struck seven o'clock, eight o'clock,
nine, ten, eleven.
The clock struck midnight
and began to glow.
The cuckoo came out
and called three times.
"Cuckoo! Cuckoo! Cuckoo!"

Clara the ragdoll jumped up
and began to dance.
"I love to dance," she sang,
as she danced around the shop.
"Look out Clara!" called Edward.
But he was too late.
Clara tripped over the sleeping Rory
and sat down with a bump.

Rory did not move.
He was fast asleep.
Only his tail twitched.
The toys laughed.
''He can sleep through anything,''
said Tom.
''What would it take to wake him?''
asked Clara.

Clara was about to start dancing
again when Flick the blue rabbit
called out, "Shh! There's something
in the shop!"
"What is it?" asked Edward.
"I don't know," said Springer,
the pink rabbit. "It's coming
towards our cushion."

All the toys listened.
At first there was nothing.
Then there was the sound
of very soft footsteps.
''Look!'' called Flick.
He pointed to the corner of
the shop.
There, the toys could see
two green, glowing eyes!

"It's Mrs Harper's cat!"
said Edward. "Quick!
Everyone onto the shelves
and out of her way!"
The toys climbed, jumped
and scrambled onto the shelves
as quickly as they could.
"What do we do now?" cried Clara.
The cat sat and looked at
the toys on the shelves.

"Let me think," said Edward.
"There is someone who can help.
We'll wake up Rory. He's a fierce lion.
He'll scare the cat away."
The toys stood around
the sleeping lion.
"We must wake him," said Tom.
He banged his big bass drum
next to Rory's ear,
Boom! Boom! Boom!
Rory slept on.

Edward had an idea.
He called the mice.
"Line up on each side of Rory's tail,"
he said. "When I say bite, you must
all bite at once!"
"It won't hurt Rory, will it?" said Clara.
"Quick," said Tom. "The cat is licking
her lips and looking at Flick!"
"Ready, steady, BITE!" shouted Edward.

Raaaaarrr!
Rory woke up with a roar!
He jumped into the air
and landed on the cat's back!
The cat screeched, "Meeoooow!"
She ran straight through the door
and upstairs, to where
Mrs Harper lived.
"Hooray!" shouted the toys.
"Hooray for Rory!"

Rory sat holding his tail.
"That hurt," he whimpered.
"You poor lion," said Clara.
"You need a bandage."
She tied a green spotted ribbon
round Rory's tail.
"Is it – is it – very bad?" asked Rory.
"You are a very brave lion," said Clara.
"Everyone will know how brave you
are when they see your bandages."
That made Rory very happy.

"I think I'll go back to sleep now,"
yawned Rory. "A lion needs his sleep."
He opened one eye. "If you need
me again," he said, "just wake
me up."
"We'll try," said the toys.
Just then dawn broke and the
toys could no longer move or talk.
Daylight shone through the window
and lit up Rory's green spotted
bandage.

Say these words again

dreamed	shelves
asleep	fierce
hero	bite
glow	bandage
bump	ribbon
cushion	brave
eyes	wake